D1222616

THE OWL-SCATTERER

For Nicholas Dybek

THE
OWL-SCATTERER

by HOWARD NORMAN

Wood Engravings by Michael McCurdy

The Atlantic Monthly Press
Boston
New York

Nov

GIFT

Upper Nyack School Library

P4482ual

Jake was old. Some folks said he was nearly one hundred. He lived alone in a cabin in the far north of Canada, near the village of Big Footprint Lake.

One winter morning Jake walked to the general store to buy eggs, flour, and tea. A few townspeople stood nearby. The store's owner, Mr. Garth Helm, said to them, "Here comes that rickety hermit, Jake! Don't get him going, all he talks about are owls!" Jake tried to act as if he didn't hear.

When he got back home he swept the snow from his porch, looking up just in time to see a snowy owl land near the edge of the woods. The snow was deep and sun glinted off it. Jake had to shade his eyes to see, but there was no mistaking a snowy owl. The owl blinked a few times, stared at Jake with its wide eyes, then —WHOOSH! — it flew away with a great sweep of its wings.

Visits from owls were special. Owls trusted Jake. He had spent long days and nights in the woods watching them. Now he recognized each owl at a glance. He knew each of their voices. Jake could even imitate how each owl flew, by making hand shadows race over the snow.

When he had finished sweeping, Jake went inside. He put on his slippers and walked into the pantry. There were boxes everywhere — stacks and stacks of them — all overflowing with owl feathers.

Jake took up a single feather and rubbed it between his fingers. "No one in the village is old enough to remember when I was the best owl-scatterer in the world," he said to himself.

Snow fell for five days. When it stopped, Jake pushed out onto his porch, hoping to see an owl.

What he *did* see was the mayor's son, Bozzie Modine.

"Bozzie Modine," Jake shouted, "why aren't you in school?"

"No school today because of the big worry," Bozzie answered.

"Haven't you heard? There are too many owls!"

"Why, that's impossible!" Jake exclaimed. "I haven't seen an owl in days. If owls were anywhere they'd be out here with me!"

"You haven't been in the village. Owls are everywhere! Come see!"

"No, no. You come back and tell me what happens."

"Jake," Bozzie said, "my great-grandfather told me that you are the best owl-scatterer in the world. Don't worry about the people in the village. Come and show them!"

Jake thought a minute, then reached for his coat.

"Well, I am curious to see all those owls," Jake said.

When they got to town the first place they stopped was the general store. Bozzie opened the door and said, "Look!"

Jake peeked in. There was a long-eared owl sitting on the counter. There was a short-eared owl on the cash register. Owls were lined up on the shelves! Mr. Garth Helm even had a hawk-owl on top of his head!

"Every shop and home in the village is full of owls!" Mr. Garth Helm said. "We don't know what to do!"

"Come along with us," Bozzie said. "There's a meeting in the town hall."

"What's *he* doing here?" Mr. Garth Helm whispered to Bozzie, pointing at old Jake.

"Just wait and see," said Bozzie.

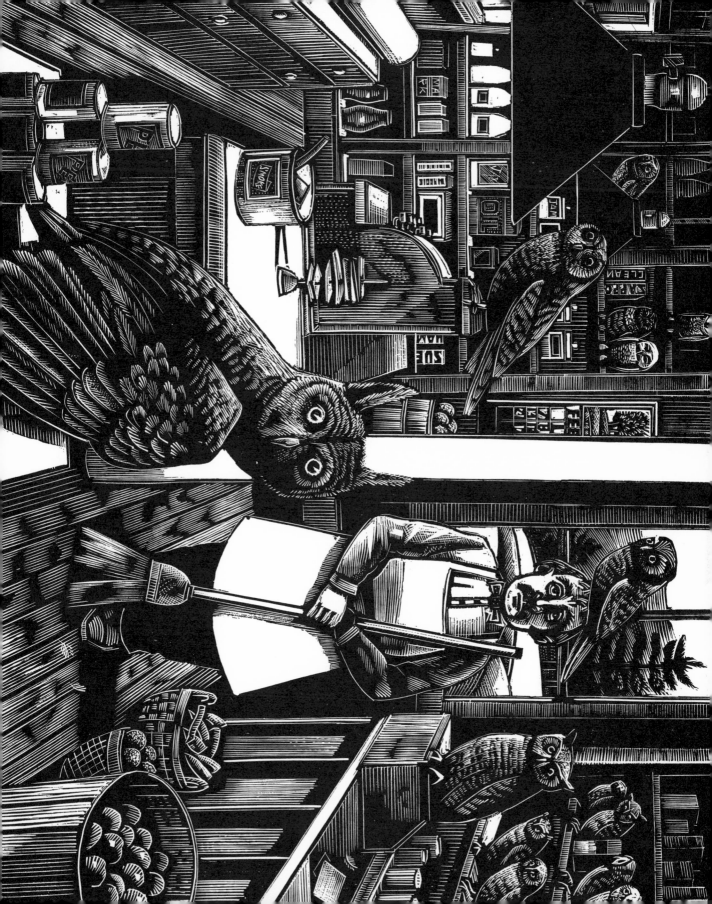

The town hall was crowded. Almost every citizen of Big Foot-print Lake was there. Jake looked up at the rafters. What a sight! All the northern owls were there. Long-eared owls sat next to short-eared owls. There were barred owls, hawk owls, saw-whet owls, and great gray owls. Jake thought he even recognized the snowy owl who had visited him a few days earlier.

Bozzie sat down next to Jake just as Bozzie's father, Mayor Chester Modine, stood up and announced, "This meeting is officially called to order!"

He tapped his wooden gavel. Suddenly the town hall came alive with owls! It was a blizzard of flapping wings, swirling feathers, and loud hooting, hooting, hooting! Even Jake, who loved owl sounds, had to cover his ears!

"Calm down, please!" the mayor begged the owls. "We can't hear a thing with all that racket!"

Jake leaned over and whispered to Bozzie, "I'm afraid the mayor doesn't quite know how to talk with owls."

"Maybe you'd better help," said Bozzie.

Jake stood up. "Hoo hoo hoo," he cried. "Hoo hoo hoo."

Within moments the air was still again.

The mayor was flustered. "As you can see," he continued, "we have a worry, a very big worry. We have too many owls. They are a nuisance. So I have asked you here to try and figure out what we should do — *oo wha oo!*"

Mayor Chester Modine sounded just like an owl himself!

"Why, excuse me!" the mayor stammered. "I really don't know how that happened. Quite embarrassing! Now, I love owls as much as anyone. And I could understand if *one* owl chose to live in our village and not out in the woods, or maybe even two — *oo wha oo!*"

"Why, I must apologize again!" said the mayor. "I think these owls are playing a trick on me!"

"Don't apologize," said Jake, winking at Bozzie. "It makes you sound very respectable and wise."

Then Jake stood up. "You're not old enough to remember when the owls used to gather right here in the village," he said, "but I am. When I was a boy, owls would visit every night to hunt mice and sit on our porches. Now they've all come back."

"Why?" asked the mayor. "Why? Why?"

"To give me my old job back, of course," said Jake. "That's why."

"Ha, ha, ha!" laughed the mayor. "You're joking!"

The words were barely out of the mayor's mouth when suddenly there was a great Whoosh! In a rush of feathers and talons a great gray owl swooped down toward the mayor, so close that the tip of its wing brushed his face. The owl turned in midair. Thump! It landed on the podium.

With its deep voice the owl boomed, "*Woo ah woo, woo ah woo.*"

All the owls began to shake their wings. Hoot! Hoot! Hoot! Thousands of feathers filled the air.

"Stop!" cried the mayor. "We'll be swimming in feathers!"

Everyone was running in circles, owl feathers sticking out of their mouths.

"Go ahead, Jake," Bozzie cried above the noise. "Now's the time. Scatter the owls!"

Jake got a wild look in his eyes. He puffed out his cheeks. He tore at his white hair.

He stretched out his arms like wings and began to whirl them, churning up a wind so strong that it put out the fire in the fireplace!

Hats and mittens swirled in the air.

Along the wall, coats lifted from wooden pegs and whizzed around like magic carpets.

The mayor's pockets turned inside out.
The wind took up a teapot and whistled it around the town hall.
"Be careful, Jake!" shouted Bozzie. "You look as if you're about to fly yourself!"

"Step back, Bozzie," Jake bellowed. "WHOO AH WOO! WHOO AH WOO! WHOO AH WOO!"

The owls flew every which way. Some even flew up the chimney!
Bozzie threw open the door and windows, and soon they filled
the sky.

Then it was quiet. A special quiet, the kind of quiet that can only happen after hundreds of flapping owls have disappeared.

Bozzie looked around. Not only were all the owls gone, but Jake was too!

Mayor Chester Modine stood up slowly. He looked around and cleared his throat. "Where's old Jake? I owe him an apology."

Mr. Garth Helm crawled out from under a table. "I guess I do too," he said.

"He's gone with the owls," said Bozzie. "But I can find him."

When Bozzie got to Jake's cabin, Jake was sitting at the kitchen table, just where Bozzie thought he'd be.

"I want to thank you. Scattering owls again was a great pleasure," said Jake. "There's something for you in the pantry, Bozzie."

"Owl feathers!" exclaimed Bozzie, opening a box.

"I've been collecting them ever since I was your age. I want you to have them. Maybe someday you'll tell your great-grandchildren that you saw old Jake the owl-scatterer at work!"

"Will you teach me to scatter owls myself?" Bozzie asked.

"Well, now, that takes practice," said Jake. "First, you have to show the owls that you care about them. You must look for owls in marshes and meadows and the rocky shores of the lakes. You must look for them on fence posts and muskrat houses. You must sit still for a long time in the dark woods until you see the eyes of an owl shine just above a branch, like two distant lanterns. It's long, hard work, Bozzie. Are you sure you want to try?"

Bozzie took up some of the boxes. Jake held open the door for him as he stepped out onto the porch.

"I'll start tonight," Bozzie said.

TEXT COPYRIGHT © 1986 BY HOWARD NORMAN
ILLUSTRATIONS COPYRIGHT © 1986 BY MICHAEL McCURDY

ALL RIGHTS RESERVED. NO PART OF THIS BOOK MAY BE REPRODUCED
IN ANY FORM OR BY ANY ELECTRONIC OR MECHANICAL MEANS INCLUDING
INFORMATION STORAGE AND RETRIEVAL SYSTEMS WITHOUT PERMISSION
IN WRITING FROM THE PUBLISHER, EXCEPT BY A REVIEWER
WHO MAY QUOTE BRIEF PASSAGES IN A REVIEW.

FIRST EDITION

Library of Congress Cataloging-in-Publication Data

Norman, Howard
  The owl-scatterer.

  Summary: The inhabitants of a small northern Canadian
village consider Jake a lazy old man but when their town
is overrun with owls only Jake knows how to scatter the birds.
  [1. Owls—Fiction. 2. Canada—Fiction] I. McCurdy,
Michael, ill. II. Title.
PZ7.N78440w 1986   [E]   85-26760
ISBN 0-87113-058-0

\#12807450

M

Published simultaneously in Canada

PRINTED IN THE UNITED STATES OF AMERICA